The Night Before Big School

E.J. Sullivan
Illustrated by
Donna Catanese

SWEETWATER
PRESS

SWEETWATER
PRESS

The Night Before Big School
Copyright © 2006 by Sweetwater Press
Produced by Cliff Road Books

ISBN-13: 978-1-58173-528-4

Printed in China

The Night Before
Big School

'Twas the night before big school, and me and
my brother, Teddy,
Were up in our room getting our school supplies ready.

We put our shoes on the rug where old Rex lay snoring,
So we could jump right in 'em
first thing in the morning.

Mom came in to snuggle
us safe in our beds,
With visions of brand new backpacks in our heads.
Then Mom got online and Dad turned on the TV,
So they could check all the latest before going
to sleep.

When down in the kitchen, I heard such a clatter–
I sprang from my bed to see what was the matter!

Around the TV and
into the nook,
I ran 'round the corner and
took a good look.

The fridge door was open—its light filled the room—
And I could see there was somebody there
    in the gloom.
There were little people, or elves, maybe animals
    in there,
Hustling and bustling from cupboard, to table,
    to chair.

Hey, it was our dog, Rex, in charge of the action!
He was telling our cats what to pick out for packin'!
He had the cats, our hamster, turtle, even our goldfish, Trey,
Packing our school supplies and lunches for the next day!

They packed sandwiches and pudding and
  fruit-flavored gummies,
They packed crayons and pencils and books and milk monies.
From the top of the pantry to the bottom of the fridge,
They even had help from our birds, Budge and Midge.

You know how you get a funny feeling
    before a big day?
Like there are butterflies inside
    that just won't go away?
That's how I felt watching our pets
    getting things ready
For the first day of school–
    I could hardly stand steady!

I pictured the teacher
coming in
that first time:
Would she be mean?
Big and scary?
Or just fine?

Would the other kids like me, or push me around?
Would I know when to talk, when to play,
   take a nap, or sit down?

I got a little scared wondering what I would do.
Maybe the whole class would go wild, like a zoo!
Then, just when I couldn't stand it any more
And yelled out for Mom–things were
suddenly just as before.

I was back in my bed! Had it all been a dream?
Rex was asleep and the cats nowhere to be seen.
I jumped out of bed—did we miss the bus?
And saw all our school things all packed up for us.

Mom and Dad in their robes were still moving real slow,
But our backpacks and lunchboxes were ready to go.
There was even a note on the table, Teddy said:
"Good luck 2 day," was what he read.

"Who wrote you that note?" Mom said, coming over.
"Didn't you?" Teddy asked, waving it at her.
That's when we noticed, where he lay by the stair,
Old Rex had a pencil tucked behind one ear.

"Happy School Days!" Mom called as we went out the door.
And I think Rex smiled as he started to snore.